The Magical Treasure Hunt

Bedtime Healing Meditation for Children

Little Blue Zen

THE MAGICAL TREASURE HUNT

Copyright@ 2024 Jo Galloway

The right of the author has been asserted to her following the copyright writing, designs and patent act of Australia.
All rights reserved. No part of this book may be reproduced, stored or transmitted by any means whether auditory, graphic, mechanical, or electronic without the written permission of the author. Unauthorised reproduction of any part of this work is illegal and is punishable by law. Unless otherwise noted, the author and the publisher make no explicit guarantees as the accuracy of the information contained in this book may differ based on individual experiences and context
ISBN: 978-1-7635801-1-4

Published by Little Blue Zen
Birdwood NSW
Printed in Australia
Cover Design: Gagan Karunachandra
Editing: Kristine Gibson
jo@littlebluezen.com
http://www.littlebluezen.com

The Magical Treasure Hunt

Bedtime Healing Meditation for Children

Jo Galloway

Your child may like other books in this series.

- The Magical Worry Balloon. Ending anxiety & worry.

- A Coat of Flying Colours. Passing your Exams.

- Bully Proof. Keeping out the Bullies.

- I am Different, I am Me.

- Angelic Dreams. Meet your Guardian Angel

- Scared of the Dark.

- I Love School.

- Bedwetting. Dry Nights.

Little Blue Zen.com

INTRODUCTION

Why Healing Meditations.

As children we make sense of our experiences based on our limited understanding and perception. We may misinterpret events or draw conclusions that form the basis of limiting beliefs that influence our entire life. These beliefs become ingrained over time, shaping our thoughts, feelings and behaviours well into adulthood unless consciously challenged.

In my work as a practising Hypnotherapist, I've found that all my clients' concerns, whether rooted in fears, feelings of inadequacy, addictive behaviours, or other challenges, trace back to their early childhood experiences, interactions, and upbringing. It's important to note that these issues don't exclusively stem from abusive or dysfunctional environments; limiting beliefs can arise from various circumstances.

Parents or caregivers wield substantial influence in shaping our perceptions of ourselves and the world around us. Remarks, criticisms, or comparisons made by family members can foster beliefs about our capabilities, worthiness, or potential. Furthermore, interactions with peers, teachers, and authority figures also contribute to the formation of these beliefs. Repeated experiences of rejection or failure can solidify beliefs such as "I'm not good enough" or "I'm unworthy of love."

This realisation ignited my passion for intervening at the source: working with children to prevent these beliefs from taking root and manifesting into significant challenges in adulthood. By addressing issues early on, we can guide children to develop into the best versions of themselves, free from the burden of limiting beliefs that could otherwise dominate their lives.

How Healing Meditation will help your child.

Teaching children meditation offers a multitude of benefits that can positively influence their daily lives and overall development. A regular mindfulness meditation practice provides valuable tools for managing stress, navigating emotions, and promoting overall well-being. Healing meditations, in particular, bolster your child's self-belief, helping to remove any resistance they may face in adulthood. This leads to a happier, more successful and fulfilling life.

Unlike traditional meditation, which often centres on relaxation, healing meditations go a step further by focusing on recovery, balance, and reprogramming a child's self-belief. These meditations use techniques such as breathing exercises, visualization, and guided imagery to not only foster deep relaxation but also reshape their mindset.

This targeted approach helps build a stronger sense of self-confidence and resilience. By integrating positive affirmations and emotional healing, healing meditations offer a distinct advantage over traditional methods, laying a powerful foundation for a child's future success and well-being.

Meditation can also be an effective part of your child's bedtime routine, helping to calm the mind and prepare the body for restful sleep. Techniques like guided imagery and deep breathing, as outlined in this book, can signal to the brain that it's time to wind down.

Sharing these calming moments at bedtime not only strengthens the bond between parent and child, but also creates a supportive and nurturing environment. It also sets a positive example, emphasizing the importance of self-care and mindfulness.

With patience and consistency, you can help your child develop a lifelong practice that supports their mental, emotional, and physical health. Give your child the gift of relaxation and imagination with this easy-to-read story designed to inspire and uplift.

The Magical Treasure Hunt

Embark on a magical journey with your little one as they venture into the world of self-discovery through "The Magical Treasure Hunt: Bedtime Healing Meditation for Children." Snuggle up tight, take a deep breath and prepare for an adventure filled with love, acceptance and confidence.

As you guide your child through a series of relaxation exercises, they'll descend a rainbow staircase to meet their most cherished friend who awaits to accompany them on a magical adventure.

Along the enchanted path, they'll uncover glittering stones inscribed with powerful messages: "I am lovable," "My body is beautiful just as it is," "I am good enough," and "I am confident."

With each stone collected, your child will embrace their unique beauty, worth and inner strength. These treasures become their constant companions, offering reassurance and encouragement in every moment.

As they bid farewell to their magical friend and drift into a peaceful sleep, they'll carry the warmth of self-love and confidence into their dreams, knowing that they are truly amazing. Join the adventure and let your child discover the magic within themselves—a journey of empowerment, affirmation and sweet dreams awaits.

Delivered in a slow, monotone voice, this story captivates and soothes. THE MAGICAL TREASURE HUNT is also available on YouTube, providing a soothing auditory experience children can enjoy at home, in the car, or anywhere they need a moment of relaxation.

Listen on YouTube

The Magical Treasure Hunt

Snuggle up my precious Little Starlight! Tonight, we're going on a magical treasure hunt.

Before we set off, let's do something really cool.

Take a big, deep breath in, and as you do, scrunch up all your muscles.

Clench your fists, curl your toes, and roll your shoulders up towards your ears.

Hold it tight... and now, breathe out and relax all your muscles.

Feel your body sinking down, melting into your warm, cozy bed.

You're laying nice and still now, so softly close your eyes.

You can see perfectly well with your eyes closed, because all little boys and girls have the most amazing imaginations.

Way better than grown-ups.

So, I want you to imagine yourself standing at the top of a set of stairs.

There are ten stairs going all the way down to the ground.

Each step is painted in all the colours of a rainbow.

They are so bright and sparkly

At the bottom of the stairs, eagerly waiting for you is your most cherished friend.

Your most favourite person in the whole wide world.

Someone you think is absolutely amazing.

You know exactly who is waiting for you.

As you look down, you see this person beaming up at you from the bottom of the stairs.

Your heart fills with excitement because you know they have something truly special waiting just for you.

So, when you're ready, let's take each step down those rainbow stairs together and go meet them, shall we?

As you leave step ten, a wave of sleepiness washes over you.

Moving onto step nine and eight, you feel yourself becoming looser and floppier.

Stepping onto step seven, you become sleepier and sleepier, even letting out a big yawn.

Travelling down to step six and five, you're now halfway to the bottom, feeling droopy and drowsy.

On step four, every sound around you makes you feel even more relaxed, like you're floating on a fluffy white cloud.

You're feeling loose, limp and wonderfully hazy!

With each step down, you're feeling incredibly drowsy and oh so tired.

You slowly reach step three, then two.

Finally, you're taking the last step now.

As you drift down, sink down, float down, your favourite person is right there, ready to greet you.

Your cherished friend tells you, "Today is a very special day.

We're going on a magical treasure hunt!

They point to a path up ahead.

There's a sign on this side of the path that says, "Follow me to the enchanted garden."

Your friend takes you by the hand, and off you go, skipping happily together along the path towards the magical garden.

It's a beautiful day; you can feel the warmth of the sun on your shoulders.

You can hear the birds singing happily in the nearby trees.

You breathe in the wonderful smells of nature.

You're feeling very happy and extremely excited.

Up ahead, you spot a big old oak tree with a small hole in the side.

The hole is just high enough that if you stand on your tippy toes, you can reach inside.

And what's this?

A sign with your name written on it, just below the hole.

Excitedly, you race up, reach up and put your hand inside the hole.

Your fingers land on something hard.

You pull out the most beautiful crystal stone, a magical treasure rock just for you.

As you hold it in your hand, you notice a message written on the bottom of the crystal.

It's been written with a glittery pen, the writing shining brightly.

The message is very special.

It says, "I am lovable."

Reading those words "I am lovable" makes your tummy feel warm and fuzzy.

You understand those words were written just for you.

You realise how truly loveable you are.

You're loveable simply because you're you.

Every day as you grow older, you become even more loveable.

And you know what? Everyone you meet thinks you're loveable too!

When you believe you're loveable, you shine a beautiful, bright light from your heart.

Other people can see and feel that radiant light, making the world a little brighter.

That's why everyone loves you so very much.

You're incredibly special and lovable.

Your friend hands you a tiny cane basket.

You pop your stone inside, carrying it with you as you continue walking.

You're feeling so very happy and excited about finding another treasure.

Further along, you spot a new sign pointing to another path leading to a wooden bridge over a little stream.

As you walk over the bridge, you notice a bright, sparkly stone lying on the edge of the water.

You hurry across the bridge, keeping your eyes glued to your treasure rock.

You reach down and pick it up.

You turn it over, and it says, "My body is beautiful just as it is."

These words make you feel all warm and fuzzy inside, too.

Now you understand that it's perfectly okay to believe that your body is beautiful just the way it is.

You realise that it's okay for your body to look different from your friends' or the people you see on TV.

You speak kind words to yourself like, "I am beautiful just the way I am".

"I like myself," and "I am beautiful inside and out."

Every day, you think, "I am beautiful, I am loveable, just being me."

You realise that what makes you special is that you're different.

And guess what? Your friends are different too, and that's totally okay.

It's actually really nice that everyone looks different from each other.

That's the way it's supposed to be.

You understand that you're beautiful on the outside, but you also see that you are beautiful on the inside, too.

With a smile, you pop your new special stone into your basket and happily continue along the path.

Up ahead, you spot a flag attached to an old wooden garden seat.

Excitedly, you race up and find an even brighter, more glittery stone resting on the seat.

You pick it up, turn it over, and see the words, "I am good enough" written in your favourite colour.

As you read these words, you understand you are enough just as you are, and that makes you smile.

When you wake up in the morning, you think, "I am enough."

When you go to school you think, "I am good enough."

When you are playing with your friends, you chose to say, "I am enough."

When you try out for new things, you remind yourself that, "you are enough".

You think I'm enough all the time and because you think you're enough, your friends think you're enough too.

This makes you so happy.

You pop your new treasure stone into your basket and continue on.

As the path steepens, your friend offers to carry your basket.

Up ahead, you spot a charming little cottage made of stones on the edge of the forest.

On the green grass out front is a large golden red box.

You and your friend race up, excited to see what is inside.

You eagerly open the lid and find another treasure nestled at the bottom of the box.

This one is the most magical treasure rock you've ever seen—bright, sparkly, and dazzling.

On the bottom, it says, "I am confident."

Confidence simply means that you like yourself.

Knowing that you are enough is the best feeling ever.

You are amazing, and you feel amazing inside too.

When you wake up in the morning, you feel excited because you're confident and happy.

At school, you feel confident to be yourself, to laugh, play, and have fun with your friends.

You feel confident in class when you're learning something new.

Confidence shines from within, making every moment brighter.

You have such a wonderful memory, and you remember everything your teacher tells you.

When you try out for a new sport or dancing, you're confident.

You love to make new friends and try new things to do.

Because you know, you are enough and so very confident.

Now, you have your four treasure stones in your basket, each with a very special message just for you.

You know you can take those four stones with you everywhere you go.

You can take them to school, to the shops, when you play sports, and to the park.

You can even take them to bed at night, placing them at the end of your bed as you sleep.

Your treasure stones go everywhere with you, reminding you of how amazing and confident you truly are.

Whenever you need a reminder of how special, beautiful, and lovable you are, you can simply reach into your pocket, touch one of your magical stones, and remember straight away:

"I am lovable."

"I am beautiful, just as I am."

"I am good enough."

"And I am confident."

These powerful special words are always with you, guiding you with love and confidence wherever you go.

As you reach the end of the pathway, you wave goodbye to your special friend.

They hand you your basket of treasure rocks and you wave them goodbye.

You'll always be excited to see them and embark on another special journey together.

Placing your basket at the end of your bed, sleep comes upon you easily.

You feel a light, floating sensation in your body as you effortlessly drift off to sleep.

Tonight, you'll dream the most magical dreams all the way until the morning light.

Goodnight, little star.

Remember, you are truly amazing.

You are loveable

You are beautiful.

You are enough.

Sweet Dreams…………..

Also by Jo Galloway

Angelic Dreams: is a tender and soothing bedtime meditation designed to help children drift peacefully to sleep. This enchanting story takes little ones on a calming journey with their very own Guardian Angel. As they settle into their cozy beds, they are gently guided through relaxing breathing exercises and imaginative visualization.

. This meditation not only helps ease the transition to sleep but also instils a sense of comfort and security that can soothe bedtime anxieties. Perfect for creating a peaceful bedtime routine, Angelic Dreams: offers a serene path to restful sleep and enchanting nighttime adventures.

www.ingramcontent.com/pod-product-compliance
Lightning Source LLC
Chambersburg PA
CBHW042356070526
44585CB00028B/2951